SECURITY

SECURITY
Poul Anderson

ÆGYPAN PRESS

Special thanks to Produced by Greg Weeks, Stephen
Blundell and the Online Distributed Proofreading
Team at http://www.pgdp.net.

Security
A publication of
ÆGYPAN PRESS

www.aegypan.com

In a world where Security is all-important, nothing can ever be secure. A mountain-climbing vacation may wind up in deep Space. Or loyalty may prove to be high treason. But it has its rewards.

*I*t had been a tough day at the lab, one of those days when nothing seems able to go right. And, of course, it had been precisely the day Hammond, the Efficiency inspector, would choose to stick his nose in. Another mark in his little notebook —— and enough marks like that meant a derating, and Control had a habit of sending derated labmen to Venus. That wasn't a criminal punishment, but it amounted to the same thing. Allen Lancaster had no fear of it for himself; the sector chief of a Project was under direct Control jurisdiction rather than Efficiency, and Control was friendly to him. But he'd hate to see young Rogers get it — the boy had been married only a week now.

To top the day off, a report had come to Lancaster's desk from Sector Seven of the Project. Security had finally cleared it for general transmission to sector chiefs — and it was the complete design of an electronic valve on which some of the best men in Lancaster's own division, Sector Thirteen, had been sweating for six months. There went half a year's work down the drain, all for nothing, and Lancaster would have that much less to show at the next Project reckoning.

He had cursed for several minutes straight, drawing the admiring glances of his assistants. It was safe enough for a high-ranking labman to gripe about Security — in fact, it was more or less expected. Scientists had their privileges.

One of these was a private three-room apartment. Another was an extra liquor ration. Tonight, as he came home, Lancaster decided to make a dent in the latter. He'd eaten at the commissary, as usual, but hadn't stayed to talk. All the way home in the tube, he'd been thinking of that whiskey and soda.

Now it sparkled gently in his glass and he sighed, letting a smile crease his lean homely face. He was a tall man, a little stooped, his clothes — uniform and mufti alike — perpetually rumpled. Solitary by nature, he was still unmarried in spite of the bachelor tax and had only one son. The boy was ten years old now, must be in the Youth Guard; Lancaster wasn't sure, never having seen him.

It was dark outside his windows, but a glow above the walls across the skyway told of the city pulsing and murmuring beyond. He liked the quiet of his evenings alone and had withstood a good deal of personal and official pressure to serve in various patriotic organizations. "Damn it," he had explained, "I'm not doing routine work. I'm on a Project, and I need relaxation of my own choosing."

He selected a tape from his library. *Eine Kleine Nachtmusik* lilted joyously about him as he found a chair and sat down. Control hadn't gotten around to making approved lists of music yet, though you'd surely never hear Mozart in a public place. Lancaster got a cigar from the humidor and collapsed his long gaunt body across chair and hassock. Smoke, whiskey, good music — they washed his mind clean of worry and frustration; he drifted off in a mist of unformed dreams. Yes, it wasn't such a bad world.

*T*he mail-tube went *ping!* and he opened his eyes, swearing. For a moment he was tempted to let the pneumo-roll lie where it fell, but habit was too strong. He grumbled his way over to the basket and took it out.

The stamp across it jerked his mind to wakefulness. *OfiSal, sEkret, fOr adresE OnlE* — and a Security seal!

After a moment he swallowed his thumping heart. It couldn't be serious, not as far as he personally was concerned anyway. If that had been the case, a squad of monitors would have been at the door. Not this message tube.... He broke the seal and unfolded the flimsy with elaborate care. Slowly, he scanned it. Underneath the official letterhead, the words were curt. *"Dis iz A matr uv urjensE and iz top sEkret. destrY Dis letr and Du tUb kontAniN it.* tUmOrO, 15 jUn, at 2130 ourz, U wil gO tU Du obzurvatOrE, A nIt klub at 5730 viktOrE strEt, and ask Du hedwAtr fOr A mistr Berg. U wil asUm Dat hE iz an Old frend uv yOrz and Dat Dis iz A sOSal EveniN. Du UZUal penaltEz ar invOkt fOr fAlUr tU komplI."

There was no signature. Lancaster stood for a moment, trying to imagine what this might be. There was a brief chill of sweat on his skin. Then he suppressed his emotions. He had nothing to fear. His record was clean and he wasn't being arrested.

His mind wandered rebelliously off on something that had occurred to him before. Admittedly the new phonetic orthography was more efficient than the old, if less esthetic; but since little of the earlier literature was being re-issued in modern spelling not too many books had actually been condemned as subversive — only a few works on history, politics, philosophy, and the like, together with some scientific texts restricted for security reasons; but one by one, the great old writings were sent to forgetfulness.

Well, these were critical times. There wasn't material and energy to spare for irrelevant details. No doubt when complete peace was achieved there would be a renaissance. Meanwhile he, Lancaster, had his Euripides and Goethe and whatever else he liked, or knew where to borrow it.

As for this message, they must want him for something big, maybe something really interesting.

Nevertheless, his evening was ruined.

*T*he Observatory was like most approved recreation spots — large and raucous, selling un-
rationed food and drink and amusement at un-
controlled prices of which the government took
its usual lion's share. The angle in this place was
astronomy. The ceiling was a blue haze a-glitter
with slowly wheeling constellations, and the
strippers began with make-believe spacesuits.
There were some rather good murals on the
walls depicting various stages of the conquest
of space. Lancaster was amused at one of them.
When he'd been here three years ago, the first
landing on Ganymede had shown a group of

men unfurling a German flag. It had stuck in his mind, because he happened to know that the first expedition there had actually been Russian. That was all right then, seeing that Germany was an ally at the time. But now that Europe was growing increasingly cold to the idea of an American-dominated world, the Ganymedean pioneers were holding a good safe Stars and Stripes.

Oh, well. You had to keep the masses happy. They couldn't see that their sacrifices and the occasional short wars were necessary to prevent another real smashup like the one seventy-five years ago. Lancaster's annoyance was directed at the sullen foreign powers and the traitors within his own land. It was because of them that science had to be strait-jacketed by Security regulations.

The headwaiter bowed before him. "I'm looking for a friend," said Lancaster. "A Mr. Berg."

"Yes, sir. This way, please."

Lancaster slouched after him. He'd worn the dress uniform of a Project officer, but he felt that all eyes were on its deplorable sloppiness. The headwaiter conducted him between tables of half-crocked customers — burly black-uniformed Space Guardsmen, army and air officers, richly clad industrialists and union bosses, civilian leaders, their wives and mistresses. The waiters were all Martian slaves, he noticed, their phosphorescent owl-eyes smoldering in the dim blue light.

He was ushered into a curtained booth. There was an auto-dispenser so that those using it need not be interrupted by servants, and an ultrasonic globe on the table was already vibrating to soundproof the region. Lancaster's gaze went to the man sitting there. In spite of being short, he was broad-shouldered and compact in plain grey evening pajamas. His face was round and freckled, almost cherubic, under a shock of sandy hair, but there were merry little devils in his eyes.

"Good evening, Dr. Lancaster," he said. "Please sit down. What'll you have?"

"Thanks, I'll have Scotch and soda." Might as well make this expensive, if the government was footing the bill. And if this —— Berg —— thought him un-American for drinking an imported beverage, what of it? The scientist lowered himself into the seat opposite his host.

"I'm having the same, as a matter of fact," said Berg mildly. He twirled the dial and slipped a couple of five-dollar coins into the dispenser slot. When the tray was ejected, he sipped his drink appreciatively and looked across the rim of the glass at the other man.

"You're a high-ranking physicist on the Arizona Project, aren't you, Dr. Lancaster?" he asked.

That much was safe to admit. Lancaster nodded.

"What is your work, precisely?"

"You know I can't tell you anything like that."

"It's all right. Here are my credentials." Berg extended a wallet. Lancaster scanned the cards and handed them back.

"Okay, so you're in Security," he said. "I still can't tell you anything, not without proper clearance."

Berg chuckled amiably. "Good. I'm glad to see you're discreet. Too many labmen don't understand the necessity of secrecy, even between different branches of the same organization." With a sudden whiplike sharpness: "You didn't tell anyone about this meeting, did you?"

"No, of course not." Despite himself, Lancaster was rattled. "That is, a friend asked if I'd care to go out with her tonight, but I said I was meeting someone else."

"That's right." Berg relaxed, smiling. "All right, we may as well get down to business. You're getting quite an honor, Dr. Lancaster. You've been tapped for one of the most important jobs in the Solar System."

"Eh?" Lancaster's eyes widened behind the contact lenses. "But no one else has informed me —"

"No one of your acquaintance knows of this. Nor shall they. But tell me, you've done work on dielectrics, haven't you?"

"Yes. It's been a sort of specialty of mine, in fact. I wrote my thesis on the theory of dielectric polarization and since then — no, that's classified."

"M-hm." Berg took another sip of his drink. "And right now you're just a cog in a computer-development Project. You see, I do know a few things about you. However, we've decided — higher up, you know, in fact on the very top level — to take you off it for the time being and put you on this other job, one concerning your specialty. Furthermore, you won't be part of a great organizational machine, but very much on your own. The fewer who know of this, the better."

Lancaster wasn't sure he liked that. Once the job was done — if he were possessed of all information on it — he might be incarcerated or even shot as a Security risk. Things like that had happened. But there wasn't much he could do about it.

"Have no fears." Berg seemed to read his thoughts. "Your reward may be a little delayed for Security reasons, but it will come in due time." He leaned forward, earnestly. "I repeat, this project is *top secret*. It's a vital link in something much bigger than you can imagine, and few men below the President even know of it. Therefore, the very fact that you've worked on it — that you've done any outside work at all

— must remain unknown, even to the chiefs of your Project."

"Good stunt if you can do it," shrugged Lancaster. "But I'm hot. Security keeps tabs on everything I do."

"This is how we'll work it. You have a furlough coming up in two weeks, don't you — a three months' furlough? Where were you going?"

"I thought I'd visit the Southwest. Get in some mountain climbing, see the canyons and Indian ruins and —"

"Yes, yes. Very well. You'll get your ticket as usual and a reservation at the Tycho Hotel in Phoenix. You'll go there and, on your first evening, retire early. Alone, I need hardly add. We'll be waiting for you in your room. There'll be a very carefully prepared duplicate — surgical disguise, plastic fingerprinting tips, fully educated in your habits, tastes, and mannerisms. He'll stay behind and carry out your vacation while we smuggle you away. A similar exchange will be affected when you return, you'll be told exactly how your double spent the summer, and you'll resume your ordinary life."

"Ummm —— well ——" It was too sudden. Lancaster had to hedge. "But look —— I'll be supposedly coming back from an outdoor vacation, with a suntan and well rested. Somebody's going to get suspicious."

"There'll be sun lamps where you're going, my friend. And I think the chance to work independently on something that really interests you will prove every bit as restful to your nerves as a summer's travel. I know the scientific mentality." Berg chuckled. "Yes, indeed."

*T*he exchange went off so smoothly that it was robbed of all melodrama, though Lancaster had an unexpectedly eerie moment when he confronted his double. It was his own face that looked at him, there in the impersonal hotel room, himself framed against blowing curtains and darkness of night. Then Berg gestured him to follow and they went down a cord ladder hanging from the windowsill. A car waited in the alley below and slid into easy motion the instant they had gotten inside.

There was a driver and another man in the front seat, both shadows against the moving blur of street lamps and night. Berg and Lancaster sat in the rear, and the secret agent chatted all the way. But he said nothing of informational content.

When the highway had taken them well into the loneliness of the desert, the car turned off it, bumped along a miserable dirt track until it had crossed a ridge, and slowed before a giant transcontinental dieselectric truck. A man emerged from its cab, waving an unhurried arm, and the car swung around to the rear of the van. There was a tailgate lowered, forming a ramp; above it, the huge double doors opened on a cavern of blackness. The car slid up the ramp, and the man outside pushed it in after them and closed the doors. Presently the truck got into motion.

"This is *really* secret!" whistled Lancaster. He felt awed and helpless.

"Quite so. Security doesn't like the government's right hand to know what its left is doing." Berg smiled, a dim flash of teeth in his shadowy face. Then he was serious. "It's necessary, Lancaster. You don't know how strong and well-organized the subversives are."

"They —" The physicist closed his mouth. It was true — he hadn't the faintest notion, really. He followed the news, but in a cursory fashion, without troubling to analyze the meaning of it. Damn it all, he had enough else to think about. Just as well that elections had been suspended and bade fair to continue indefinitely in abeyance. If he, a member of the intelligentsia, wasn't sufficiently acquainted with the political and military facts of life to make rational decisions, it certainly behooved the ill-educated masses to obey.

"We might as well stretch ourselves," said the driver. "Long way to go yet." He climbed out and switched on an overhead light.

*T*he interior of the van was roomy, even allowing for the car. There were bunks, a table and chairs, a small refrigerator and cookstove. The driver, a lean saturnine man who seemed to be forever chewing gum, began to prepare coffee. The other sat down, whistling tunelessly. He was young and powerfully built, but his right arm ended in a prosthetic claw. All of them were dressed in inconspicuous civilian garb.

"Take us about ten hours, maybe," said Berg. "The spaceship's 'way over in Colorado."

He caught Lancaster's blank stare, and grinned. "Yes, my friend, your lab is out in space. Surprised?"

"Mmm — yeah. I've never been off Earth."

"Sokay. We run at acceleration, you won't be spacesick." Berg drew up a chair, sat down, and tilted it back against a wall. The steady rumble of engines pulsed under his words:

"It's interesting, really, to consider the relationship between government and military technology. The powerful, authoritarian governments have always arisen in such times as the evolution of warfare made a successful fighting machine something elaborate, expensive, and maintainable by professionals only. Like in the Roman Empire. It took years to train a legionnaire and a lot of money to equip an army and keep it in the field. So Rome became autarchic. However, it was not so expensive a proposition that a rebellious general couldn't put some troops up for a while — or he could pay them with plunder. So you did get civil wars. Later, when the Empire had broken up and warfare relied largely on the individual barbarian who brought his own weapons with him, government loosened. It had to — any ruler who got to throwing his weight around too much would have insurrection on his hands. Then as war again became an art — well, you see how it goes. There are other factors, of course, like religion — ideology in general. But by and large, it's worked out the way I explained it. Because there are always people willing to fight when government encroaches on what they consider their liberties, and governments are always going to try to encroach. So the balance struck depends on comparative strength. The American colonists back in 1776 relied on citizen levies and weapons were so cheap and simple that almost anyone could obtain them. Therefore government stayed loose for a long time. But nowadays, who except a government can make atomic bombs and space rockets? So we get absolute states."

*L*ancaster looked around, feeling the loneliness close in on him. The driver was still clattering the coffee pot. The one-armed man was utterly blank and expressionless. And Berg sat there, smiling, pouring out those damnable cynicisms. Was it some kind of test? Were they probing his loyalty? What kind of reply was expected?

"We're a democratic nation and you know it," he said. It came out more feebly than he had thought.

"Oh, well, sure. This is just a state of emergency which has lasted unusually long, seventy-two years to be exact. If we hadn't lost World War III, and needed a powerful remilitarization to overthrow the Soviet world — but we did." Berg took out a pack of cigarettes. "Smoke? I was just trying to explain to you why the subversives are so dangerous. They have to be, or they wouldn't stand any kind of chance. When you set out to upset something as big as the United States government, it's an all or nothing proposition. They've had a long time now to organize, and there's a huge percentage of malcontents to help them out."

"Malcontents? Well, look, Berg — I mean, you're the expert and of course you know your business, but a natural human grumble at conditions doesn't mean revolutionary sentiments. These aren't such bad times. People have work, and their needs are supplied. They aren't hankering to have the Hemispheric Wars back again."

"The standard revolutionary argument," said Berg patiently, "is that the rebels aren't trying to overthrow the nation at all, but simply to restore constitutional and libertarian govern-ment. It's common knowledge that they have help and some subsidies from outside, but it's contended that these are merely countries tired of a world dominated by an American dictator-ship and, being small Latin-American and European states, couldn't possibly think of con-quering us. Surely you've seen subversive litera-ture."

"Well, yes. Can't help finding their pam-phlets. All over the place. And —" Lancaster closed his mouth. No, damned if he was going to admit that he knew three co-workers who listened to rebel propaganda broadcasts. Those were silly, harmless kids — why get them in trouble, maybe get them sent to camp?

"You probably don't appreciate the hold that kind of argument has on all too many intellectuals — and a lot of the common herd, too," said Berg. "Naturally you wouldn't — if your attitude has always been unsympathetic, these people aren't going to confide their thoughts to you. And then there are bought men, and spies smuggled in, and — oh, I needn't elaborate. It's enough to say that we've been thoroughly infiltrated, and that most of their agents have absolutely impeccable dossiers. We can't give neoscop to everybody, you know — Security has to rely on spot checks and the testing of key personnel. Only when organizations get as big as they are today, there's apt to be no real key man, and a few spies strategically placed in the lower echelons can pick-up a hell of a lot of information. Then there are the colonists out on the planets — our hold on them has always necessarily been loose, because of transportation and communication difficulties if nothing else. And, as I say, foreign powers. A little country like Switzerland or Denmark or Venezuela can't do much by itself, but an undercover international pooling of resources. . . . Anyway, we have reason to believe in the existence of a large, well financed, well organized underground, with trained fighting men, big secret weapons dumps, and saboteurs ready for the word 'go' — to say nothing of a restless population and any number of covert sympathizers who'd follow if the initial uprising had good results."

"Or bad, depending on whose viewpoint you take," grinned the one-armed man.

Lancaster put his elbows on his knees and rested his forehead on shaking hands. "What has all this got to do with me?" he protested. "I'm not the hero of some cloak-and-dagger spy story. I'm no good at undercover stuff — what do you want of me?"

"It's very simple," Berg replied quietly. "The balance of power is still with the government, because it does have more of the really heavy weapons than any other group can possibly muster. Alphabet bombs, artillery, rockets, armor, spaceships and space missiles. You see? Only research has lately suggested that a new era in warfare is developing — a new weapon as decisive as the Macedonian phalanx, gunpowder, and aircraft were in their day." As Lancaster raised his eyes, he met an almost febrile glitter in Berg's gaze. "And *this* weapon may reverse the trend. It may be the cheap and simple arm that anyone can make and use — the equalizer! So we've got to develop it before the rebels do. They have laboratories of their own, and their skill at stealing our secrets makes it impossible for us to trust the research to a Project in the usual manner. The fewer who knew of this weapon, the better — because in the wrong hands it could mean — Armageddon!"

*T*he run from Earth was short, for the space laboratory wasn't far away at the moment as interplanetary distances go. Lancaster wasn't told anything about its orbit, but guessed that it had a path a million miles or so sunward from Earth and highly tilted with respect to the ecliptic. That made for almost perfect concealment, for what spaceship would normally go much north or south of the region containing the planets?

He was too preoccupied during the journey to estimate orbital figures, anyway. He had seen enough pictures of open space, and some of them had been excellent. But the reality towered unbelievably over all representations. There simply is no way of describing that naked grandeur, and when you have once experienced it you don't want to try. His companions — Berg and the one-armed Jessup, who piloted the spaceboat — respected his need for silence.

The station had been painted non-reflecting black, which complicated temperature control but made accidental observation of its existence almost impossible. It loomed against the cold glory of stars like a pit of ultimate darkness, and Jessup had to guide the boat in with radar. When the last lock had clanged shut behind him and he stood in a narrow metal corridor, shut away from the sky, Lancaster felt a sense of unendurable loss.

It faded, and he grew aware of others watching him. There were half a dozen people, a motley group dressed in any shabby garment they happened to fancy, with no sign of the semi-military discipline of a Project crew. A Martian hovered in the background, and Lancaster didn't notice him at first. Berg introduced the humans casually. There was a stocky grey-haired man named Friedrichs, a lanky space-tanned young chap called Isaacson, a middle-aged woman and her husband by the name of Dufrere, a quiet Oriental who answered to Hwang, and a red-haired woman presented as Karen Marek. These, Berg explained, were the technicians who would be helping Lancaster. This end of the space station was devoted to the labs and factories; for security reasons, Lancaster couldn't be permitted to go elsewhere, but it was hoped he would be comfortable here.

"Ummm — pardon me, aren't you a rather mixed group?" asked the physicist.

"Yes, very," said Berg cheerfully. "The Dufreres are French, Hwang is Chinese, and Karen here is Norwegian though her husband was Czech. Not to mention. . . . There you are, I didn't see you before! Dr. Lancaster, I'd like you to meet Rakkan of Thyle, Mars, a very accomplished labman."

*L*ancaster gulped, shifting his feet and looking awkwardly at the small grey-feathered body and the beaked owl-face. Rakkan bowed politely, sparing Lancaster the decision of whether or not to shake the clawlike hand. He assumed Rakkan was somebody's slave — but since when did slaves act as social equals?

"But you said this project was top secret!" he blurted.

"Oh, it is," smiled Karen Marek. She had a husky, pleasant voice, and while she was a little too thin to be really good-looking, she was cast in a fine mold and her eyes were large and grey and lovely. "I assure you, non-Americans are perfectly capable of preserving a secret. More so than most Americans, really — we don't have ties on Earth. No one to blab to."

"It's not well known today, but the original Manhattan Project that constructed the first atomic bombs had quite an international character," said Berg. "It even included German, Italian, and Hungarian elements though the United States was at war with those countries."

"Come along and we'll get you settled in your quarters," invited Isaacson.

Lancaster followed him down the long hallways, rather dazed with the whole business. He noticed that the space station had a crude, unfinished look, as if it had been hastily thrown together from whatever materials were available. That didn't ring true for a government enterprise, no matter how secret.

Berg seemed to read his thought again. "We've worked under severe handicaps," he said. "Look, just suppose a lot of valuable material and equipment were ferried into space. If it's an ordinary government deal, you know how many light-years of red tape are involved. Requisitions have to be filled out in triplicate, every last rivet has to be accounted for — there'd simply have been too much chance of a rebel spy getting a lead on us. It was safer all around to use whatever chance materials could be obtained from salvage or through individual purchases on other planets. Ever hear of the *Waikiki?*"

"Ummm — seems so — wasn't she the big freighter that disappeared many years ago?"

"That's the one. A meteor swarm struck her on the way to Venus. Furthermore, one of them shorted out her engine controls, so that she swooped out of the ecliptic plane and fell into an eccentric skew orbit. When this project was first started, one of our astronomers thought he'd identified the swarm — it has a regular path of its own about the sun, though the orbit is so cockeyed that spaceships hardly ever even see the things. Anyway, knowing the orbit of the meteors and that of the *Waikiki* at the time, he could calculate where the disaster must have taken place —— which gave us a lead in searching for the hulk. We found it after a lot of investigation, moved it here, and built the station up around it. Very handy. And completely secret."

Lancaster had always suspected that Security was a little mad. Now he knew it. Oh, well ——

*H*is room was small and austere, but privacy was nice. The lab crew ate in a common refectory. Beyond the edge of their territory, great bulkheads blocked off three-fourths of the space station. Lancaster was sure that many people and several Martians lived there, for in the days that followed he saw any number of strangers appearing and disappearing in the region allowed him. Most of these were workmen of some kind or other, called in to help the lab crew as needed, but all of them were tight-lipped. They must have been cautioned not to speak to the guest more than was strictly necessary.

Living was Spartan in the station. It rotated fast enough to give weight, but even on the outer skin that was only one-half Earth gravity. A couple of silent Martians prepared undistinguished meals and did housework in the quarters. There were no films or other organized recreation, though Lancaster was told that the forbidden sector included a good-sized room for athletics.

But the crew he worked with didn't seem to mind. They had their own large collections of books and music wires, which they borrowed from each other. They played chess and poker with savage skill. Conversation was, at first, somewhat restrained in Lancaster's presence, and most of the humor had so little reference to things he knew that he couldn't follow it, but he became aware that they talked with more animation and intelligence than his friends on Earth. Manners were utterly informal, and it wasn't long before even Lancaster was being addressed by his first name; but cooperation was smooth and there seemed to be none of the intrigue and backbiting of a typical Project crew.

And the work filled their lives. Lancaster was caught up in it the "day" after his arrival, realized at once what it meant, and was plunged into the fascination of it. Berg hadn't lied; this was big!

The perfect dielectric.

Such, at least, was the aim of the project. It was explained to Lancaster that one Dr. Sophoulis had first seen the possibilities and organized the research. It had gone ahead slowly, hampered by a lack of needed materials and expert personnel. When Sophoulis died, none of his assistants felt capable of carrying on the work at any decent rate of speed. They were all competent in their various specialties, but it takes more than training to do basic research — a certain inborn, intuitive flair is needed. So they had sent to Earth for a new boss — Lancaster.

The physicist scratched his head in puzzlement. It didn't seem right that something so important should have to take the leavings of technical personnel. Secrecy or not, the most competent men on Earth should have been tapped for this job, and they should have been given everything they needed to carry it through. Then he forgot his bewilderment in the clean chill ecstasy of the work.

Man had been hunting superior dielectrics for a long time now. It was more than a question of finding the perfect electrical insulator, though that would be handy too. What was really important was the sort of condensers made possible by a genuinely good dielectric material. Given that, you could do fantastic things in electronics. Most significant of all was the matter of energy storage. If you could store large amounts of electricity in an accumulator of small volume, without appreciable leakage loss, you could build generators designed to handle average rather than peak load — with resultant savings in cost; you could build electric motors, containing their own energy supply and hence portable —— which meant electric automobiles and possibly aircraft; you could use inconveniently located power sources, such as remote waterfalls, or dilute sources like sunlight, to augment —— maybe eventually replace —— the waning reserves of fuel and fissionable minerals; you could. . . . Lancaster's mind gave up on all the possibilities opening before him and settled down to the immediate task at hand.

"The original mineral was found on Venus, in the Gorbu-vashtar country," explained Karen Marek. "Here's a sample." She gave him a lump of rough, dense material which glittered in hard rainbow points of light. "It was just a curiosity at first, till somebody thought to test its electrical properties. Those were slightly fantastic. We have all chemical and physical data on this stuff already, of course, as well as an excellent idea of its crystal structure. It's a funny mixture of barium and titanium compounds with some rare earths and — well, read the report for yourself."

Lancaster's eyes skimmed down the sheaf of papers she handed him. "Can't make very good condensers out of this," he objected. "Too brittle — and look how the properties vary with temperature. A practical dielectric has to be stable in every way, at least over the range of conditions you intend to use it in."

She nodded.

"Of course. Anyway, the mineral is very rare on Venus, and you know how tough it is to search for anything in Gorbu-vashtar. What's important is the lead it gave Sophoulis. You see, the dielectric constant of this material isn't constant at all. It *increases* with applied voltage. Look at this curve here."

Lancaster whistled. "What the devil — but that's impossible! That much variability means a crystal structure which is — uh — flexible, damn it! But you've got a brittle substance here —"

According to the accepted theory of dielectricity, this couldn't be. Lancaster realized with a thumping behind his veins that the theory would have to be modified. Rather, this was an altogether different phenomenon from normal insulation.

He supposed some geological freak had formed the mineral. Venus was a strange planet anyway. But that didn't matter. The important thing now was to get to know this process. He went off into a happy mist of quantum mechanics, oscillation theory, and periodic functions of a complex variable.

Karen and Isaacson exchanged a slow smile.

Sophoulis and his people had done heroic work under adverse conditions. A tentative theory of the mechanism involved had already been formulated, and the search had started for a means to duplicate the super-dielectricity in materials otherwise more suitable to man's needs. But as he grew familiar with the place and the job, Lancaster wondered just how adverse the conditions really were.

True, the equipment was old and cranky, much of it haywired together, much of it invented from scratch. But Rakkan the Martian, for all his lack of formal education, was unbelievably clever where it came to making apparatus and making it behave, and Friedrichs was a top-flight designer. The lab had what it needed — wasn't that enough?

The rest of Lancaster's crew were equally good. The Dufreres were physical chemists *par excellence*, Isaacson a brilliant crystallographer with an unusual brain for mathematics, Hwang an expert on quantum theory and inter-atomic forces, Karen an imaginative experimenter. None of them quite had the synthesizing mentality needed for an overall picture and a fore-vision of the general direction of work — that had been Sophoulis' share, and was now Lancaster's — but they were all cheerful and skilled where it came to detail work and could often make suggestions in a theoretical line.

Then, too, there was no Security snooping about, no petty scramble for recognition and promotion, no red tape. What was more important, Lancaster began to realize, was the personal nature of the whole affair. In a Project, the overall chief set the pattern, and it was followed by his subordinates with increasingly less latitude as you worked down through the lower ranks. You did what you were told, produced results or else, and kept your mouth shut outside your own sector of the Project. You had only the vaguest idea of what actually was being created, and why, and how it fitted into the broad scheme of society.

Hwang and Rakkan commented on that, one "evening" at dinner when they had grown more relaxed in Lancaster's presence. "It was inevitable, I suppose, that scientific research should become corporate," said the Chinese. "So much equipment was needed, and so many specialties had to be coordinated, that the solitary genius with only a few assistants hadn't a chance. Nevertheless, it's a pity. It's destroyed initiative in many promising young men. The top man is no longer a scientist at all — he's an administrator with some technical background. The lower ranks do have to exercise ingenuity, yes, but only along the lines they are ordered to follow. If some interesting sideline crops up, they can't investigate it. All they can do is submit a memorandum to the chief, and most likely if anything is done it will be carried out by someone else."

"What would you do about it?" shrugged Lancaster. "You just admitted that the old-time genius in a garret can't compete."

"No — but the small team of creative specialists, each with an excellent understanding of the others' fields, and each working in a loose, free-willed cooperation with the rest, can. Indeed, the results will be much better. It was tried once, you may know. The early cybernetics men, back in the last century, worked that way."

"I wish we could co-opt some biologists and psychologists into this," murmured Rakkan. His English was good, though indescribably accented by his vocal apparatus. "The cellular and neural implications of dielectricity look — promising. Maybe later."

"Well," said Lancaster defensively, "a large Project can be made more secure — less chance of leakage."

Hwang said nothing, but he cocked an eyebrow at an almost treasonable angle.

*I*n going through Sophoulis' equations, Lancaster found what he believed was the flaw that was blocking progress. The man had used a simplified quantum mechanics without correction for relativistic effects. That made for neater mathematics but overlooked certain space-time aspects of the psi function. The error was excusable, for Sophoulis had not been familiar with the Belloni matrix, a mathematical tool that brought order into what was otherwise incomprehensible chaos. Belloni's work was still classified information, being too useful, in the design of new alloys, for general consumption.

Lancaster went happily to work correcting the equations. But when he was finished, he realized that he had no business showing his results without proper clearance.

He wandered glumly into the lab. Karen was there alone, setting up an apparatus for the next attempt at heat treatment. A smock covered her into shapelessness, and her spectacular hair was bound up in a kerchief, but she still looked good. Lancaster, a shy man, was more susceptible to her than he wanted to be.

"Where's Berg?" he asked.

"Back on Earth with Jessup," she told him. "Why?"

"Damn! It holds up the whole business till he returns." Lancaster explained his difficulty.

Karen laughed. "Oh, that's all right," she said in the low voice he liked to hear. "We've all been cleared."

"Not officially. I've got to see the papers."

She glared at him then and stamped her foot. "How stupid can you get without having to be spoon fed?" she snapped. "You've seen how much we think of regulations here. Let's have those equations, Mac."

"But — blast it, Karen, you don't appreciate the need for security. Berg explained it to me once — how dangerous the rebels are, and how easily they can steal our secrets. And they'll stop at nothing. Do you want another Hemispheric War?"

She looked oddly at him, and when she spoke it was softly. "Allen, do you really believe that?"

"Certainly! It's obvious, isn't it? Our country is maintaining the peace of the Solar System — once we drop the reins, all hell will run away from us."

"What's wrong with setting up a worldwide federation of countries? Most other nations are willing."

"But that — it's not *practical!*"

"How do you know? It's never been tried."

"Anyway, we can't decide policy. That's just not for us."

"The United States is a democratic country — remember?"

"But —" Lancaster looked away. For a moment he stood unspeaking, and she watched him with grave eyes and said nothing. Then, not really knowing why he did it, he lifted a defiant head. "All right! We'll go ahead — and if Berg sends us all to camp, don't blame me."

"He won't." She laughed and clapped his shoulder. "You know, Allen, there are times when I think you're human after all."

"Thanks," he grinned wryly. "How about — uh — how about having a — a b-beer with me now? To celebrate."

"Why, sure."

*T*hey went down to the shop. A cooler of beer was there, its contents being reckoned as among the essential supplies brought from Earth by Jessup. Lancaster uncapped two bottles, and he and Karen sat down on a bench, swinging their legs and looking over the silent, waiting machines. Most of the station personnel were off duty now, in the arbitrary "night."

He sighed at last. "I like it here."

"I'm glad you do, Allen."

"It's a funny place, but I like it. The station and all its wacky inhabitants. They're heterodox as the very devil and would have trouble getting a dog catcher's job back home, but they're all refreshing." Lancaster snapped his fingers. "Say, that's it! That's why you're all out here. The government needs your talents, and you aren't quite trusted, so you're put here out of range of spies. Right?"

"Do you have to see a rebel with notebook in hand under every bed?" she asked with a hint of weariness. "The First Amendment hasn't been repealed yet, they say. Theoretically we're all entitled to our own opinions."

"Okay, okay, I won't argue politics. Tell me about some of the people here, will you? They're an odd bunch."

"I can't tell you much, Allen. That's where Security does apply. Isaacson is a Martian colonist, you've probably guessed that already. Jessup lost his hand in a — a fight with some enemies once. The Dufreres had a son who was killed in the Moroccan incident." Lancaster remembered that that affair had involved American power used to crush a French spy ring centered in North Africa. Sovereignty had been brushed aside. But damn it, you had to preserve the status quo, for your own survival if nothing else. "Hwang had to go into exile when the Chinese government changed hands a few years back. I —"

"Yes?" he asked when her voice faded out.

"Oh, I might as well tell you. My husband and I lived in America after our marriage. He was a good biotechnician and had a job with one of the big pharmaceutical companies. Only he — went to camp. Later he died or was shot, I don't know which." Her words were flat.

"That's a shame," he said inadequately.

"The funny part of it is, he wasn't engaged in treason at all. He was quite satisfied with things as they were — oh, he talked a little, but so does everybody. I imagine some rival or enemy put the finger on him."

"Those things happen," said Lancaster. "It's too bad, but they happen."

"They're bound to occur in a police state," she said. "Sorry. We weren't going to argue politics, were we?"

"I never said the world was perfect, Karen. Far from it. Only what alternative have we got? Any change is likely to be so dangerous that — well, man can't afford mistakes."

"No, he can't. But I wonder if he isn't making one right now. Oh, well. Give me another beer."

They talked on indifferent subjects till Karen said it was her bedtime. Lancaster escorted her to her apartment. She looked at him curiously as he said good night, and then went inside and closed the door. Lancaster had trouble getting to sleep.

*T*he corrected equations provided an adequate theory of super-dielectricity — a theory with tantalizing hints about still other phenomena — and gave the research team a precise idea of what they wanted in the way of crystal structure. Actually, the substance to be formed was only semi-crystalline, with plastic features as well, all interwoven with a grid of carbon-linked atoms. Now the trick was to produce that stuff. Calculation revealed what elements would be needed, and what spatial arrangement — only how did you get the atoms to assume the required configuration and hook up in the right way?

Theory would get you only so far, thereafter it was cut and try. Lancaster rolled up his sleeves with the rest and let Karen take over the leadership — she was the best experimenter. He spent some glorious and all but sleepless weeks, greasy, dirty, living in a jungle of haywired apparatus with a restless slide rule. There were plenty of failures, a lot of heartbreak and profanity, an occasional injury — but they kept going, and they got there.

The day came — or was it the night? — when Karen took a slab of darkly shining substance out of the furnace where it had been heat-aging. Rakkan sawed it into several chunks for testing. It was Lancaster who worked on the electric properties.

He applied voltage till his generator groaned, and watched in awe as meters climbed and climbed without any sign of stopping. He discharged the accumulated energy in a single blue flare that filled the lab with thunder and ozone. He tested for time lag of an electric signal and wondered wildly if it didn't feel like sleeping on its weary path.

The reports came in, excited yells from one end of the long, cluttered room to the other, exultant whoops and men pounding each other on the back. This was it! This was the treasure at the rainbow's end.

*T*he substance and its properties were physically and chemically stable over a temperature range of hundreds of degrees. The breakdown voltage was up in the millions. The insulation resistance was better than the best known to Earth's science.

The dielectric constant could be varied at will by a simple electric field normal to the applied voltage gradient — a field which could be generated by a couple of dry cells if need be — and ranged from a hundred thousand to about three billion. For all practical purposes, here was the ultimate dielectric.

"We did it!" Friedrichs slapped Lancaster's back till it felt that the ribs must crack. "We have it!"

"Whooppee!" yelled Karen.

Suddenly they had joined hands and were dancing idiotically around the induction furnace. Lancaster clasped Rakkan's talons without caring that it was a Martian. They sang then, sang till heads appeared at the door and the glassware shivered.

Here we go 'round the mulberry bush,
The mulberry bush, the mulberry bush —

It called for a celebration. The end of a Project meant no more than filing a last report and waiting for the next assignment, but they ran things differently out here. Somebody broke out a case of Venusian aguacaliente. Somebody else led the way to a storeroom, tossed its contents into the hall, and festooned it with used computer tape. Rakkan forgot his Martian dignity and fiddled for a square dance, with Isaacson doing the calling. The folk from the other end of the station swarmed in till the place overflowed. It was quite a party.

Hours later, Lancaster was hazily aware of lying stretched on the floor. His head was in Karen's lap and she was stroking his hair. The hardy survivors were following the Dufreres in French drinking songs, which are the best in the known universe. Rakkan's fiddle wove in and out, a lovely accompaniment to voices that were untrained but made rich and alive by triumph.

"Sur ma tomb' je veux qu'on inscrive:
'Ici-git le roi des buveurs.'
Sur ma tomb' je veux qu'on inscrive:
'Ici-git le roi des buveurs.
Ici-git, oui, oui, oui,
Ici-git, non, non, non ———'"

Lancaster knew that he had never been really happy before.

*B*erg showed up a couple of days later, looking worried. Lancaster's vacation time was almost up. When he heard the news, his eyes snapped gleefully and he pumped the physicist's hand. "Good work, boy!"

"There are things to clean up yet," said Lancaster, "but it's all detail. Anybody can do it."

"And the material —— what do you call it, anyway?"

Karen grinned. "So far, we've only named it *ffuts*," she said. "That's 'stuff' spelled backward."

"Okay, okay. It's easy to manufacture?"

"Sure. Now that we know how, anybody can make it in his own home — if he's handy at tinkering apparatus together."

"Fine, fine! Just what was needed. This is the ticket." Berg turned back to Lancaster. "Okay, boy, you can pack now. We blast again in a few hours."

The physicist shuffled his feet. "What are my chances of getting re-assigned back here?" he asked. "I've liked it immensely. And now that I know about it anyway —"

"I'll see. I'll see. But remember, this is top secret. You go back to your regular job and don't say a word on this to anyone less than the President — no matter what happens, understand?"

"Of course," snapped Lancaster, irritated. "I know my duty."

"Yeah, so you do." Berg sighed. "So you do."

Leavetaking was tough for all concerned. They had grown fond of the quiet, bashful man — and as for him, he wondered how he'd get along among normal people. These were his sort. Karen wept openly and kissed him good-bye with a fervor that haunted his dreams after-ward. Then she stumbled desolately back to her quarters. Even Berg looked glum.

He regained his cockiness on the trip home, though, and insisted on talking all the way. Lancaster, who wanted to be alone with his thoughts, was annoyed, but you don't insult a Security man.

"You understand the importance of this whole business, and why it has to be secret?" nagged Berg. "I'm not thinking of the scientific and industrial applications, but the military ones."

"Oh, sure. You can make lightning throw-ers if you want to. And you've overcome the fuel problem. With a few *ffuts* accumulators, charged from any handy power source, you can build fuelless military vehicles, which would simplify your logistics immensely. And some really deadly handguns could be built — pistols the equivalent of a cannon, almost." Lancaster's voice was dead. "So what?"

"So plenty! Those are only a few of the applications. If you use your imagination, you can think of dozens more. And the key point is —— the *ffuts* and the essential gadgetry using it are cheap to make in quantity, easy to handle —— the perfect weapon for the citizen soldier. Or for the rebel! It isn't enough to decide the outcome of a war all by itself, but it may very well be precisely the extra element which will tip the military balance against the government. And I've already discussed what that means."

"Yes, I remember. That's your department, not mine. Just let me forget about it."

"You'd better," said Berg.

*I*n the month after his return, Lancaster lived much as usual. He was scolded a few times for an increasing absent-mindedness and a lack of enthusiasm on the Project, but that wasn't too serious. He became more of an introvert than ever. Having some difficulty with getting to sleep, he resorted to soporifics and then, in a savage reaction, to stimulants. But outwardly there was little to show the turmoil within him.

He didn't know what to think. He had always been a loyal citizen — not a fanatic, but loyal — and it wasn't easy for him to question his own basic assumptions. But he had experienced something utterly alien to what he considered normal, and he had found the strangeness more congenial —— more human in every way — than the norm. He had breathed a different atmosphere, and it couldn't but seem to him that the air of Earth was tainted. He re-read Kipling's *Chant-Pagan* with a new understanding, and began to search into neglected philosophies. He studied the news in detail, and his critical eye soon grew jaundiced —— did this editorial or that feature story have any semantic content at all, or was it only a tom-tom beat of loaded connotations? The very statements of fact were subject to doubt —— they should be checked against other accounts, or better yet against direct observation; but other accounts were forbidden and there was no chance to see for himself.

He took to reading seditious pamphlets with some care, and listened to a number of underground broadcasts, and tried clumsily to sound out those of his acquaintances whom he suspected of rebellious thoughts. It all had to

be done very cautiously, with occasional night-
mare moments when he thought he was being
spied on; and was it right that a man should be
afraid to hear a dissenting opinion?

He wondered what his son was doing. It
occurred to him that modern education existed
largely to stultify independent thought.

At the same time, he was unable to dis-
card the beliefs of his whole life. Sedition was
sedition and treason was treason — you
couldn't evade that fact. There were no more
wars — plenty of minor clashes, but no real
wars. There was a stable economy, and nobody
lacked for the essentials. The universal state
might be a poor solution to the problems of a
time of troubles, but it was nevertheless a solution. Change would be unthinkably dangerous.

Dangerous to whom? To the entrenched
powers and their jackals. But the oppressed peo-
ples of Earth had nothing to lose, really, except
their lives, and many of them seemed quite
willing to sacrifice those. Did the rights of man
stop at a full belly, or was there more?

He tried to take refuge in cynicism. After all, he was well off. He was a successful jackal. But that wouldn't work either. He required a more basic philosophy.

One thing that held him back was the thought that if he became a rebel, he would be pitted against his friends — not only those of Earth, but that strange joyous crew out in space. He couldn't see fighting against them.

Then there was the very practical consideration that he hadn't the faintest idea of how to contact the underground even if he wanted to. And he'd make a hell of a poor conspirator.

He was still in an unhappy and undecided whirlpool when the monitors came for him.

*T*hey knocked on the door at midnight, as was their custom, and he felt such an utter panic that he could barely make it across the apartment to let them in. The four burly men wavered before his eyes, and there was a roaring and a darkness in his head. They arrested him without ceremony on suspicion of treason, which meant that habeas corpus and even the right of trial didn't apply. Two of them escorted him to a car, the other two stayed to search his dwelling.

At headquarters, he was put in a cell and left to stew for some hours. Then a pair of men in the uniform of the federal police led him to a questioning chamber. He was given a chair and a smiling, soft-voiced man — almost fatherly, with his plump cheeks and white hair — offered him a cigarette and began talking to him.

"Just relax, Dr. Lancaster. This is pretty routine. If you've nothing to hide then you've nothing to fear. Just tell the truth."

"Of course." It was a dry whisper.

"Oh, you're thirsty. So sorry. Alec, get Dr. Lancaster a glass of water, will you, please? And by the way, my name is Harris. Let's call this a friendly conference, eh?"

Lancaster drank avidly. Harris' manner was disarming, and the physicist felt more at ease. This was — well, it was just a mistake. Or maybe a simple spot check. Nothing to fear. He wouldn't be sent to camp — not he. Such things happened to other people, not to Allen Lancaster.

"You've been immunized against neoscop?" asked Harris.

"Yes. It's routine for my rank and over, you know. In case we should ever be kidnapped

— but why am I telling *you* this?" Lancaster tried to smile. His face felt stiff.

"Hm. Yes. Too bad."

"Of course, I've no objection at all to your using a lie detector on me."

"Fine, fine." Harris beamed and gestured to one of the expressionless policemen. A table was wheeled forth, bearing the instrument. "I'm glad you're so cooperative, Dr. Lancaster. You've no idea how much trouble it saves me — and you."

They ran a few harmless calibrating questions. Then Harris said, still smiling, "And now tell me, Dr. Lancaster. Where were you really this summer?"

Lancaster felt his heart leap into his throat, and knew in a sudden terror that the dials were registering his reaction. "Why — I took my vacation," he stammered. "I was in the Southwest —"

"Mmmm — the machine doesn't quite agree with you." Harris remained impishly cheerful.

"But it's *true!* You can check back and —"

"There are such things as doubles, you know. Come, come, now, let's not waste the whole night. We both have many other things to do."

"I — look." Lancaster gulped down his panic and tried to speak calmly. "Suppose I am lying. The machine should tell you that I'm not doing so out of disloyalty. There are things I can't tell anyone without clearance. Like if you asked me about my work on the Project — I can't tell you that. Why don't you check through regular Security channels? There was a man named Berg — at least he called himself that. You'll find that it's all perfectly okay with Security."

"You can tell me anything," said Harris gently.

"I can't tell you this. Not anybody short of the President." Lancaster caught himself. "Of course, that's assuming that I did really spend the summer for something other than my vacation. But —"

Harris sighed. "I was afraid of this. I'm sorry, Lancaster." He nodded to his policemen. "Go ahead, boys."

*L*ancaster kept sliding into unconsciousness. They jolted him back to life with stimulant injections and vigorous slaps and resumed working on him. Now and then they would let up and Harris' face would swim out of a haze of pain, smiling, friendly, sympathetic, offering him a smoke or a shot of whiskey. Lancaster sobbed and wanted more than anything else in the world to do as that kindly man asked. But he didn't dare. He knew what happened to those who revealed state secrets.

Finally he was thrown back into his cell and left to himself. When he recovered from his faint — that was a very slow process — he had no idea of how many hours or days had gone by. There was a water tap in the room and he drank thirstily, vomited the liquid up again, and sat with his head in his hands.

So far, he thought dully, they hadn't done too much to him. He was short several teeth, and there were some broken fingers and toes, and maybe a floating kidney. The other bruises, lacerations, and burns would heal all right if they got the chance.

Only they wouldn't.

He wondered vaguely how Security had gotten onto his track. Berg's precautions had been very thorough. So thorough, apparently, that Harris could find no trace of what had really happened that summer, and was going only on suspicion. But what had made him suspicious in the first place? An anonymous tip-off — from whom? Maybe some enemy, some rival on the Project, had chosen this way of getting rid of his sector chief.

In the end, Lancaster thought wearily, he'd tell. Why not do it now? Then — probably — he'd only be shot for betraying Berg's confidence. That would be the easy way out.

No. He'd hang on for awhile yet. There was always a faint chance.

His cell door opened and two guards came in. He was past flinching from them, but he had to be supported on his way to the questioning room.

Harris sat there, still smiling. "How do you do, Dr. Lancaster," he said politely.

"Not so well, thank you." The grin hurt his face.

"I'm sorry to hear that. But really, it's your own fault. You know that."

"I can't tell you anything," said Lancaster. "I'm under Security oath. I can't speak of this to anyone below the President."

Harris looked annoyed. "Don't you think the President has better things to do than come running to every enemy of the state that yaps after him?"

"There's been some mistake, I tell you," pleaded Lancaster.

"I'll say there has. And you're the one that's made it. Go ahead, boys." Harris picked up a magazine and started reading.

*A*fter awhile, Lancaster focused his mind on Karen Marek and kept it there. That helped him bear up. If they knew, out in the station, what was happening to him, they — well, they wouldn't forget him, try to pretend they'd never known him, as the little fearful people of Earth did. They'd speak up, and do their damnedest to save their friend.

The blows seemed to come from very far away. They didn't do things like this out in the station. Lancaster realized the truth at that moment, but it held no surprise. The most natural thing in the world. And now, of course, he'd never talk.

Maybe.

When he woke up, there was a man before him. The face blurred, seemed to grow to monstrous size and then move out to infinite distances. The voice of Harris had a ripple in it, wavering up and down, up and down.

"All right, Lancaster, here's the President. Since you insist, here he is."

"Go ahead, American," said the man. "Tell me. It's your duty."

"No," said Lancaster.

"But I am the President. You wanted to see me."

"Most likely a double. Prove your identity."

The man who looked like the President sighed and turned away.

*L*ancaster woke up again lying on a cot. He must have been brought awake by a stimulant, for a white-coated figure was beside him, holding a hypodermic syringe. Harris was there too, looking exasperated.

"Can you talk?" he asked.

"I — yes." Lancaster's voice was a dull croak. He moved his head, feeling the ache of it.

"Look here, fellow," said Harris. "We've been pretty easy with you so far. Nothing has happened to you that can't be patched up. But we're getting impatient now. It's obvious that you're a traitor and hiding something."

Well, yes, thought Lancaster, he was a traitor, by one definition. Only it seemed to him that a man had a right to choose his own loyalties. Having experienced what the police state meant, he would have been untrue to himself if he had yielded to it.

"If you don't answer my questions in the next session," said Harris, "we'll have to start getting really rough."

Lancaster remained silent. It was too much effort to try to speak.

"Don't think you're being heroic," said Harris. "There's nothing pretty or even very human about a man under interrogation. You've been screaming as loud as anybody."

Lancaster looked away.

He heard the doctor's voice. "I'd advice giving him a few days' rest before starting again, sir."

"You're new here, aren't you?" asked Harris.

"Yes, sir. I was only assigned to this duty a few weeks ago."

"Well, we don't put on kid gloves for traitors."

"That's not what I mean, sir," said the doctor. "There are limits to pain beyond which further treatment simply doesn't register. Also, I'm a little suspicious about this man's heart. It has a murmur, and questioning puts a terrific strain on it. You wouldn't want him to die on your hands, would you, sir?"

"Mmmm — no. What do you advise?"

"Just a few days in the hospital, with treatment and rest. It'll also have a psychological effect as he thinks of what's waiting for him."

Harris considered for a moment. "All right. I've got enough other things to do anyway."

"Very good, sir. You won't regret this."

Lancaster heard the footsteps retreat into silence. Presently the doctor came around to stand facing him. He was a short, curly-haired man of undistinguished appearance. For a mo-

ment they locked eyes, then Lancaster closed
his. He wanted to tell the doctor to go away, but
it wasn't worth the trouble.

Later he was put on a stretcher and carried down endless halls to another cell. This one
had a hospital look about it, somehow, and the
air was sharp with the smell of antiseptics. The
doctor came when he was installed in bed and
took his arm and slipped a needle into it.
"Sleepy time," he said.

Lancaster drifted away again.

When he woke up, he felt darkness and movement. He looked around, wondering if he had gone blind, and the breath moaned out between his bruised lips. A hand was laid on his shoulder and a voice spoke out of the black.

"It's okay, fella. Take it easy. There'll be no more questions."

It was the doctor's voice, and the doctor looked nothing at all like Charon, but still Lancaster wondered if he weren't being ferried over the river of death. There was a thrumming all about him, and he heard a low keening of wind. "Where are we going?" he mumbled.

"Away. You're in a stratorocket now. Just take it easy."

Lancaster fell asleep after awhile.

Beyond that there was a drugged, confused period where he was only dimly aware of moving and trying to talk. Shadows floated across his vision, shadows telling him something he couldn't quite grasp. He followed obediently enough. Full clarity came eventually, and he was lying in a bunk looking up at a metal ceiling. The shivering pulse of rockets trembled in his body. A spaceship?

A spaceship!

He sat up, heart thudding, and looked wildly around. "Hey!" he cried.

The remembered figure of Berg came through the door. "Hullo, Allen," he said. "How're you feeling?"

"I — you —" Lancaster sank weakly back to his pillow. He grew aware that he was thoroughly bandaged, splinted, and braced, and that there was no more pain. Not much, anyway.

"I feel fine," he said.

"Good, good. The doc says you'll be okay." Berg sat down on the edge of the bunk. "I can't stay here long, but the hell with it. We'll be at the station soon. You deserve to know some things, such as that you've been rescued."

"Well, that's obvious," said Lancaster.

"By us. The rebels. The underground. Subversive characters."

"That's obvious too. And thanks ——" The word was so ridiculously inadequate that Lancaster had to laugh.

"*I* suppose you've guessed most of it already," said Berg. "We needed a scientist of your caliber for our project. One thing we're desperately short of is technical personnel, since the only real education in such lines is to be had on Earth and most graduates find comfortable berths in the existing society. Like you, for instance. So we played a trick on you. We used part of our organization — yes, we have a big one, and it's pretty smart and powerful too — to convince you this was a government job of top secrecy. More damn things can be done in the name of Security —" Berg clicked his tongue. "Everybody you saw at the station was more or less play-acting, of course. The whole thing was set up to fool you. We might not have gotten away with it if we'd used some other person, more shrewd about such things, but we'd studied you and knew you for an amiable, unsuspicious guy, too wrapped up in your own work to go witch-smelling."

"I guessed that much," admitted Lancaster. "After I'd been in the cells for awhile. Your way of living and thinking was so different from anything like —"

"Yeah. I'm sorry as hell about that, Allen. We thought you could just return to ordinary life, but somehow — through one of those accidents or malices inevitable in a state where every man spies on his neighbor — you were hauled in. We knew of it at once — yes, we've even infiltrated the secret police — and decided to do something about it. Quite apart from the danger of your betraying what you knew — we could have eliminated that by quietly murdering you — there was the fact that we'd gotten you into this and did owe you something. We managed to get Dr. Pappas transferred to the inquisitory where you were being held. He drugged you, producing a remarkably corpselike figure, and smuggled you out as simply another one who'd died under questioning. I used my Security papers to get the body for special autopsy instead of the usual immediate cremation. Then we simply drove till we reached the stratorocket we'd arranged to have ready, and you were flown to our spaceboat, and now you're on the way back to the station. You were kept under drugs most of the way to help you rest — they'd knocked you around quite a bit in the inquisitory. So —" Berg shrugged. "Pappas can't go back to Earth now, of course, but we can always use a medic in space, and it was well worth the trouble to rescue you."

"I'm honored," said Lancaster.

"I still feel like hell about what happened to you, though."

"It's all right. I can't say I enjoyed it, but now that I've learned some hard facts — oh, well, forget the painful nature of the lesson. I'll be okay. And I'm going home!"

*J*essup supported Lancaster as they entered the space station. His old crew was there waiting to greet him. They were all immensely pleased to have him back, though Karen wept bitterly on his shoulder.

"It's all right," he told her. "I'm not in such bad shape as I look. Honest, Karen, I'm all right. And now that I have gotten back, and know where I really belong — damn, but it was worth it!"

She looked at him with eyes as grey as a rainy dawn. "And you are with us?" she whispered. "You're one of us? Of your own will?"

"Of course I am. Give me a week or two to rest, and I'll be back in the lab bossing all of you like a Simon Legree. Hell, we've just begun on that super-dielectricity. And there are a lot of other things I want to try out, too."

"It means exile," she said. "No more blue skies and green valleys and ocean winds. No more going back to Earth."

"Well, there are other planets, aren't there? And we'll go back to Earth in the next decade, I bet. Back to start a new American Revolution and write the Bill of Rights in the sky for all to see." Lancaster grinned shyly. "I'm not much at making speeches, and I certainly don't like to listen to them. But I've learned the truth and I want to say it out loud. The right of man to be free is the most basic one he's got, and when he gives that up he finishes by surrendering everything else too. You people are fighting to bring back honesty and liberty and the possibility of progress. I hope nobody here is a fanatic, because fanaticism is exactly what we're fighting against. I say we, because from now on

I'm one of you. That is, if you're sure you want me."

He stopped, clumsily. "Okay. Speech ended."

Karen drew a shivering breath and smiled at him. "And everything else just begun, Allen," she said. He nodded, feeling too much for words.

"Get to bed with you," ordered Pappas.

*J*essup led Lancaster off, and one by one the others drifted back to their jobs. Finally only Karen and Berg stood by the airlock.

"You keep your beautiful mouth shut, my dear," said the man.

"Oh, sure." Karen sighed unhappily. "I wish I'd never learned your scheme. When you explained it to me I wanted to shoot you."

"You insisted on an explanation," said Berg defensively. "When Allen was due to go back to Earth, you wanted us to tell him who we were and keep him. But it wouldn't have worked. I've studied his dossier, and he's not the kind of man to switch loyalties that easily. If we were to have him at all, it could only be with his full consent. And now we've got him."

"It was still a lousy trick," she said.

"Of course it was. But we had no choice. We *had* to have a first-rate physicist."

"You know," she said, "you're a rat from way back."

"That I am. And by and large, I enjoy it." Berg grimaced. "Though I must admit this job leaves a bad taste in my mouth. I like Allen. It was the hardest thing I ever did, tipping off the federal police about him."

He turned on his heel and walked away, smiling faintly.

www.ingramcontent.com/pod-product-compliance
Lightning Source LLC
Chambersburg PA
CBHW050803250626

47155CB00005B/2193